This edition first published in the United
Kingdom in 2012 by Pavilion Children's Books
10 Southcombe Street
London, W14 0RA

Design and layout © 2012 Pavilion Children's Books
Text and illustrations © 2012 Frann Preston-Gannon

ISBN: 978-1-84365-209-0

A CIP catalogue record for this book is available from the British Library.

10 9 8 7 6 5 4 3 2 1

Reproduction by Mission Productions Ltd, Hong Kong
Printed and bound by Toppan Leefung, China

This book can be ordered directly from the publisher online at
www.anovabooks.com

For my Mother
and Father.

The journey home

Frann Preston-Gannon

PAVILION
CHILDREN'S

The frozen sea was melting. 'Where has all of my ice gone?' the Polar Bear wondered. 'And where is my food?' He looked around. 'Well, I can't stay here,' he decided, so he went for a swim.

As he swam along he found a little boat, alone upon the sea.

'This will be easier than swimming,' he thought as he climbed in.

Before long he came upon a city where machines rumbled and tall buildings hid the sky.

'What are you doing?' asked a Panda
watching from the docks.

'I am sailing in my boat,' replied the
Polar Bear, 'it's easier than swimming,
you see.'

'Well, I can't stay here,' said the Panda
lowering himself down into the boat.
'I think I'll come with you.'

And together the two animals sailed along,
listening to the seagulls and saying hello to the fish.

After a while, they floated up a river to where a jungle used to be. 'I've nothing to climb anymore,' said an Orang-utan. 'My trees are disappearing.'

The Panda and the Polar Bear looked around and saw that she was right.

'Well, you could join us if you like?' said the Panda. 'Perhaps we will spot some trees along the way.' So she climbed in and off they went.

As they sailed on, they looked up at the sky and saw the beautiful shapes the clouds had made.

'What's that behind the rock?' said the Orang-utan suddenly.

'Shsshhh...' said an Elephant. 'I'm trying to hide. Someone's trying to steal my tusks.'

'Why don't you come with us?' whispered the Panda. 'We can sail far away from here.'

So the Elephant climbed in too.

And so the animals laughed and played as their small boat carried them further and further. But the sea started to swell and dark clouds appeared in the sky.

The storm
passed and the animals
knew the terrible waves had carried
them far far away. They thought of their
homes and how much they missed
them. As they sailed on they
all felt very lost on the
big blue sea.

A Dodo watched from his island as the boat and its animals came into view. 'Hello there!' he called to them as they sailed closer.

'We're lost!' shouted the
Polar Bear to the Dodo.
'We've sailed too far and now
we want to go home.'

'Well of course you can
go home!' said the Dodo.

'Really?' said the animals together.
'When?'

'You can go home when
the trees grow back
and when the ice returns
and when the cities stop
getting bigger and
when the hunting stops.'

'Oh,' said the Orang-utan
thoughtfully.

'And when will that be?' asked the Polar Bear.

'I don't know,' said the Dodo.
'Let's see what tomorrow brings.'

MEET THE CREW

The Polar Bear's home is under threat. The arctic is getting warmer because of climate change and the sea ice where he feeds is melting away.

Elephants are often killed by poachers for their tusks which are made of ivory. Habitat loss is also threatening their future.

The Orang-utan is losing its home. It lives in forests but due to over-logging for wood its home is getting smaller and smaller.

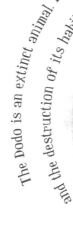

The Panda only eats bamboo and because of the destruction of its natural home it is harder and harder for it to find the food it needs.

The Dodo is an extinct animal. Due to over-hunting and the destruction of its habitat there are no Dodos left.